# ON HER REVERIE

A FICTIONAL FAIRYTALE

RAMAKANT

First published by Writer's Pocket in 2026

email: editor@writerspocket.com



Cover Design by Ramakant



ISBN-13: 978-93-344-1108-9



www.writerspocket.com

# TABLE OF CONTENTS -

# ABOUT THE AUTHOR ~

I mean there's nothing particularly that much special about me. I'm just a simple guy who loves to read and write about fictional things to live out the dreams that I can't in reality.

As for where I'm from, so I come from Orai, the city of King Mahil, A quite popular city of District Jalaun, Uttar Pradesh, India.

And just so you know, I wasn't always like this, not until I met Her...

Something about her made me look at myself more differently, like maybe I wasn't as lost as I used to think I was. I mean, she made me feel seen. She came into my life like a quiet storm, turning everything upside down in a quiet and gentle way. Everything started to change little by little from the day I met her.

And you know what, she didn't just make me feel something, she literally kinda stirred something inside my soul, something that I never knew existed in me.

She made me believe that I am worthy too, worthy of dreams, worthy of love and worthy of everything that I had once convinced myself I could never have. And I mean before her I was like just existing, but after her, I started living...

## INTRODUCTION ~

This debut book about Her 'On Her Reverie' is a collection of such prose and poetries that gives shape to a fictional love story of mine, a story written through imagination...

Every verse and every line in this book have been written with both dreams and ache, both presence and absence, and with love across every page. These mere words are nothing but a soft confession to someone who's the most dearest to me.

You know what, this book is written for a Girl, whom I have never truly met, yet she feels like a person I have always dreamed of. Someone who holds the most special place in my life, I mean not as a partner or a lover, but as a Soulful Friend to me...

I know, for some peoples it might not be that much worthy to read, but for me it is something that I have done for Her.

I remember, I've read somewhere that for once in your life you should feel the love of a poet or an artist, and if you're lucky to find it, they will make you immortal. Maybe that's not always true!

And, I neither know nor I care what they say because as per my opinion having A Muse Like Her is something that I could call Luck. Perhaps, that makes me a Lucky person...

But I know I'm not lucky, I'm blessed to have Her!

And you know,
I was never a poet, and never I wished to be.
But the urge to write for Her,
So that Her name never fades, made me one...

She is both the inspiration and the creation of my poems...

And, it might seem to be a coincidence, that every poem I've ever written literally makes a perfect rhyme, but believe me it's not!

It is so because of the divine perfection of that girl,
Who is My Muse!

At last, all I could say her is,

My Beloved Ruth,

You are dearer to me more than myself. You complete the parts of me I didn't knew were missing. I can't tell in words how much you mean to me. Your innocence, your kindness and your spark have quietly and completely changed the course of my life.

You've made my world brighter just by being in it. I mean, what you have given to me have made a real difference in me and my life too.

You are the poem my heart has always been trying to write.
and no matter what happens, I'm always here for you.

It seems like an honour to have You as my Muse.
To be true, I am nothing sans Thee!
And without you, there is no poetry...

Forever yours
~ *Ramakant*

*Wanna know more about Her?*

*She is the dream I cannot forget, and*
*the poem too that I'm still trying to write...*

# A GLIMPSE OF THE POEM ~

Do wishes ever come true? Some may agree, some may not.

Well, if they really do come true, what would you ask for? I know most people would wish for money or materialistic things. But what could be the greatest desire someone could make?

I guess Love!

Because a heart's deepest need is to be seen, to be loved by someone and never be left alone. These verses written down describes the need of love that is beyond the imagination...

I mean even if we know that our wish might not come true, we make it anyway, because it gives us comfort.

And in my interpretation, this poem isn't merely about magic or just fate, it's mainly all about the power of hope, and how sometimes, even the simple act of wishing can be enough to shape the course of our journey...

# POETRY 01 ~ A WISH FOR A SOULMATE

I wish I was dead!

But do wishes ever come true?

Well, if they do,

I'd have wished something new...

Something like friends,

To enjoy every moment I'd spend,

But I don't think, they'll be here,

With me, till the world's end...

Or maybe something more than friends,

Maybe a soulmate who'd make me complete,

Who'd love me more than anyone else,

Till my heart does loses its beat...

The one who'll see me through my silence,

And will hold me when the world will fall apart,

The one who'll not run from the chaos I carry,

But will stand steady, from heart to heart...

Maybe she'll find me one evening,
When the stars will forget to shine,
And will offer me more than a moment,
Maybe a promise or a sign...

I just wish I could hold onto hope till then,
That somewhere, she's searching too,
Wishing for someone like me,
Who'll turn her grey skies blue...

But until that dream arrives,
I'll walk through these nights alone,
While cradling this wish inside my chest,
Cuz all I'm left with is grief to atone...

# A GLIMPSE OF THE POEM ~

The title 'Mi Cielo' refers to a Spanish word that means 'My Heaven' or 'My Sky'. It is used as a tender expression of love and comfort which is full of emotions and warmth.

And I call her 'Mi Cielo' because:

"She is also like the sky above me, the one who lights up my days, calms my anxiety, and surrounds me in endless beauty."

Actually, for me, these two words holds galaxies within them...

It's a name I gave to someone brighter than sunshine, someone softer than moonlight, someone who made me feel alive again, someone who became my whole universe.

You know, my love for her is too big, too beautiful, and too limitless to be captured fully in these mere words.

This poem is just a small attempt to capture the immensity of what I feel for her, of what she means to me. But I know it will fall short. I mean how could these tiny syllables describe the divine?

But still, I gave a try...

# POETRY 02 ~ MI CIELO

I wish to write her immortal,
But she's already a fairy.
In my dull and gloomy life,
She’s like my sage clary...

The whole literature doesn't have
a single metaphor that could
portray the elegance of her eyes.
Though this body is in abyss,
Yet the heart feels like a paradise...

The stars and the galaxies are nothing,
Just scattered dust compared to them.
They are as a sea shore with endless rage,
Just as the waves condemn...

Their brownish hue makes me faint,
The heart wishes to drown in them.
I either start losing all my senses,
Or might began to forget who I am...

Mind says to escape the matrix,
But this dumb heart is caught
and trapped by her serene smile.
And just to have a stargaze with her,
I can live an eternity in exile...

And you know what,
Even time halts when she speaks,
Each word feels like a spell, casting peace.
Which turns the moments to soft echoes,
Through which my pain do quietly cease...

She is like some poetic verses,
Like a poem only the moon understands.
And I, a broken and ink-stained soul,
Longs to touch the lines written by her hands...

Her laughter is like a melody,
As a quiet hymn that outshines the dawn.
Or a music that lingers in the silence,
Even after when she's gone...

So let the world remain a chaos outside,

For I've found my cosmos in her gaze.

Let the stars burn and galaxies too fade away,

Cuz she's the only light that I'll ever chase...

For if one day I vanished,

From this cruel world's atmosphere,

Knew that I lived a lifetime...

Just by simply loving Her...

## A GLIMPSE OF THE POEM ~

So, this is something that I first wrote for her.

I mean the title itself speaks about her angelic beauty, her sparkling charm and of how she filled my monochrome world with many vibrant hues. It might not rhyme or make a rhythm, but these few paragraphs actually forced me to write more for her. They were like the stepping stone of my journey to capture her essence in poetry and to make her timeless in poetic verses...

And guess what, I personally feel like that sometimes we should have taken that step otherwise all that remains is just regret...

# POETRY 03 ~ A FAIRYTALE

It's time to say something about her,
but how should I start?

How do I capture her innocence,
her serene smile,
her irresistible laughter,
her kindness,
and everything she embodies?
Though I am a poet,
I can't even portray the oceanic hue in her eyes...

Her smile feels like the end of me!
And I'm not a warrior anymore,
Cuz I've already surrendered to her eyes...
She's like the color to my black and white life,
the missing piece in my puzzled existence...

And you know, If I were to learn every language,
I would still not find enough words to describe her beauty...
In fact, there aren't enough pages or ink to write about her!

But I yearn for it, and I will do it for sure.

I'll write for her till my hands start bleeding,

Till my heart says to stop,

Until the very end of time!

I know that Wishing doesn't make it happen.

All I could do is wait, and I'll wait till my last breath!

You know Dear,

In someone's eyes, you might be a canvas,

But in mine, you're a colorful masterpiece...

Sometimes I feel like I don't have a love line

because I know that you will never be mine...

Still, I close my eyes and imagine how beautiful it would be,

If we were together, all alone,

roaming somewhere, holding our hands...

And I’m not sure if it was fate,

or luck or something else,

maybe it was a coincidence,

maybe destiny, or perhaps something

that only God understands...

All I know is that I thank Him every day
for this precious gift of our meeting
that He has given to me...

And at last,
For You,
If I could, I would...
I will give up everything I have...
I will sacrifice myself too...
Just for a mere glimpse of Yours...

# POETRY 04 ~ WHEN I SAW HER FOR THE FIRST TIME

Dated ~ 12th January

The first time at 12:54 am, she sent me a black & white pic.
The first thing I noticed was her gorgeous eyes.
Those eyes literally hallucinated me...
She stated "I have dark circles. What's beautiful in them?"

But I wrote ~
"They are like a pond with sparkling lotus flowers,
swimming is something I've never mastered,
but still this silly heart wishes to get drown in them!"

Then I noticed her serene smile and her shiny flowing tresses...
This time, the heart whispered ~
"Who dreams a Roman empire?
sitting with you under a shady bower,
prancing around a park while holding your hands,
staring at you, while you gaze at the moon
is more than enough for me."

And you know what,

I didn't even knew what I was doing that night,

I mean I felt like I did lose all my senses,

like something strange have happened to me.

She felt like an angel, one without a wand, yet so divine...

I felt like she literally had bewitched my soul.

And just know she really did...

Then at 02:07 am, she wished me good luck for the next day's test, But the heart was busy writing for her!

I mean I was never a poet,

but I wanted to write her eternal.

So, I became one through penning these lines for her ~

"My soul may seem a little quite,

But my love for you is infinite..."

# A GLIMPSE OF THE POEM ~

As you can see the title, I call her My Messy Muse.

Well, this poem too is about her, the one who always inspires me in the most unexpected ways. She isn't just beautiful; she's smart and full of life, also a little delusional in many ways…

She's like an art in its rawest form, yet so bold and breathtaking…

Her tangled thoughts makes her perfect to be a poem.
Indeed, She is one. One that I can never complete!

# POETRY 05 ~ MY MESSY MUSE

So, there's a girl,
Winsome and sassy,
But she always like,
To make things messy...

She looks so smart,
Like easy on the eye,
With an alluring face,
That makes my heart fly...

Her beauty is eternal,
Not once in a blue moon,
But a shining splendor,
That forever will bloom...

Her feathery black tresses,
And those ocean deep eyes,
Feels like a fairy's charm,
This heart can't disguise...

Her irresistible laughter,

Seems like a melody...

A quiet harmony,

That sets my worries free...

She walks like poetry,

Written in the flowing breeze,

And even a little time spent with her,

Puts my tangled soul at ease...

Dear,

You speak with a spark,

That sets fire to my thoughts,

Actually, in more simple words,

You do untangle my knots...

You do colour my days,

With your whimsical hue,

And even silence feels sweet,

When I'm talking with you...

And if life is a canvas,
Then you are my art,
And you're the artist too,
Who painted my heart...

And I don't know if it's fate,
Or just a twist of time,
But you've become my reason,
My rhythm, and my rhyme...

So, here's my confession,
Simple and true...
I do feel loved
Just by being with you...

And with you by my side,
Is where I'll always wish to be,
And even if you'll ask or not,
I am just in love with Thee...!!!

## A GLIMPSE OF THE POEM ~

I guess this poem doesn't need an explanation. But here's a little something anyway.

It's still untitled, because I haven't found the perfect name for it till now. Actually, it seems impossible to me.

It's also about that girl, who's like a real-life Princess. She's kind, she's smart, and she's so full of dreams just like all those fictional princesses we all grew up hearing about.

And you know what, she is a real one and she's literally the prettiest among all of them. She too loves to read fictional things like me, explore ideas, and she brings so much light into my life.

Thinking of her makes everything feel so magical...

# POETRY 06 ~ UNTITLED

I've found a girl,
Gorgeous and exquisite,
As diligent as Cinderella,
That lights up the night...

She's an avid reader,
Always loves to read,
Just like princess Belle,
From the beauty and the beast...

She turns my anxiety,
Into fun and delight,
Kinda optimistic and innocent,
As pretty as princess Snow White...

An escapist daydreamer,
She also loves to hike,
So smart and so fearless,
Princess Rapunzel alike...

She’s compassionate and adventurous,
Having a fairy's charm with splendid grace,
Though she's like Jasmin,
Forbidden to leave the palace...

But she's also brave,
Willing to dream beyond the walls,
With a voice like Ariel's,
Who answers the ocean’s calls...

She moves with elegance,
And also speaks with fire,
Just like queen Elsa,
With quiet strength and icy desire...

Her laughter’s like a melody,
So pure and so sincere,
Just like Aurora’s hum,
That brings up the forest near...

And guess what?

She needs no kingdom,

No magic spell or even a crown,

She already holds royalty in her spirit,

And she's the prettiest in her town...

She isn't made of fantasy,

But something more far beyond,

A girl who lights up my darkness,

Just by simply being around...

So, though I call her a princess,

She's even more, you see...

She's the author of my story,

And literally the bestest part of me...

And, here's my final whisper,

As simple as it may be,

She isn't just my Love,

She's my whole destiny...

# A GLIMPSE OF THE POEM ~

By the way what's love for you?

A wish, a crave, or something having more depth than this?

Well, I don't have an exact answer. Maybe it's something that doesn't make you feel empty, like something that shows up quiet and steady, and doesn't always need words to be known. It's not always perfect or dramatic, it's just real.

In hope that this raw poetry might describe some of it...

# POETRY 07 ~ LOVE

What is love?

A realm to live?

Finding her wasn't,

But I think having her is!

It's a whispered crave,

And an unsaid dream,

It all began swiftly,

Like a rushing stream...

In every breath,

And in every sigh,

She’s an unrequited wish,

That's never gonna die...

Though time may fade,

And seasons might change,

My love for her,

Is never gonna wane...

She’s the moon and I'm just a star,
I'd rather admire her from afar!

So, what is love?
Something wild or wise,
Or a quiet forever,
In someone’s eyes...

For me, it’s Her,
And who she is in every way...
No more words required
I guess there to say...

It’s in how she sees the world,
With wonder in her eyes,
And how she brings me peace,
When she doesn’t even realize...

She’s not a part of my story,
She is the story herself!
The only meaning of love
That I’ll ever need...

Now no questions or doubts,

She's what love is all about...

And though she may never know,

Or feel the same for me,

She'll forever be the heartbeat,

Of me and my silent poetry...

## A GLIMPSE OF THE POEM ~

This piece is a letter I wish I could send to the moon.

A silent witness to all the emotions we bury deep inside us. It talks about those moments when you feel too much but you have no one to share it with, so at last you end up whispering your heart into the night.

It's written for the dreamers, the lonely souls, and the ones who send silent prayers into the sky in a hope that they're being heard.

And guess what? I too am one of them...

# POETRY 08 ~ A LETTER TO THE MOON

Dear Moon,

Do you feel the weight
of holding the unspoken stories
of those countless souls each night?
Do you ever feel sad
of observing the tender scenes of human lives?
Do you even get tired of watching all this?

The silent lovers...
The souls still searching for something,
The lonely stargazers,
Those who whisper their secrets to the sky
because they have no one else to tell?

I also lie among them,
I too have sent you letters in my dreams,
Folded them in sighs,
And sealed them
with my fragile love...

Do they ever reach you?

Or do they get drifted away

by the breeze of the stars,

or do they get lost

in the hush of midnight?

I mean it's okay

if they don't reach to you...

But, if our souls

are somehow connected,

Just send me a sign

a small shimmer in the sky,

or a soft whisper in the wind...

Just something small to say

saying I'm not alone here...

Because even a soul like mine

tired, quiet, and broken

still believes

in the magic of the moon...

And you know what, sometimes I wonder...
That do you ever wish to speak back?
Or reach down from the sky
and comfort the one who's breaking...

By the way,
if you could write me back,
Would you say you've seen me?
Or heard me?

Would you tell me
that even the quietest love
still matters
in the vastness of the night?

Because I've loved in silence too long...
I've cried without tears,
And hoped without words...
And yet,
I still look up every night,
Trusting that you're listening...

So,

If you hear me tonight,

Please send me a breeze

through my window,

move a star just slightly,

or let the night bloom

with a soft kind of light...

Just something small...

just to remind me

that even if

no one else sees me,

you do...

Always watching.

Always there...

*~ A Heartless Soul*

# A GLIMPSE OF THE POEM ~

Hey, have you ever dreamed of super powers?

Well, at first, I used to wish to be Spiderman... But I don't desire anything nowadays. I mean all I could dream now is to help people or to make their life easier a little bit just by doing something.

This small piece of poetry is a reflection of that quiet wish, I had for her at some point of life to be more than just a human, just to make her happy in a better way.

That day I wished for superpowers to help her forget her anxiety, her loneliness, her depression, and everything that made her feel sad and hopeless.

But guess what, it's just a myth... because the greatest superpower existing in this universe is neither sorcery nor a witchcraft magic.

It's Love. Just pure Love...

And that's all that I have for her...

# POETRY 09 ~ I WISH I HAD SUPER POWERS

My Dear,

I wish I had super powers,
I would have destroyed
your sorrow in just one stroke...

But all I have is pure genuine love,
So, I'll just drape your gloom
and misery in an invisible cloak...

I wish I had super powers,
I'll let you have the apricity,
So, you'll see it all as a dream
that you just had woke...

Or I would have taken you to halcyon,
So that your heartbreaking tale
have passed just as a joke...

I wish I had super powers,

I'd rewrite the stars above your sky,

And etch comfort in every word you spoke...

Or I'd do hold time still in your laughter,

And let the hope rise from every teardrop

that down your gentle cheek once broke...

I wish I had super powers,

So, I'll get appeared there,

whenever I'll hear my name that you spoke...

Either I would have taken you to feel

the universe's greatest petrichor,

Or to have a visit in the biggest garden of oak...

# A GLIMPSE OF THE POEM ~

This is one of my most favourite poems ever written by me.

It's all about love and love only, a connection so deep, that goes beyond this world into dreams, into eternity, into a place where souls do belong...

It's like a promise, like a quiet vow made to meet someone beyond the limits of time and space.

This poem kind of capture dreams, of sometime, a somewhere, a someday, where and when we'll find each other again even if we're far apart now...

## POETRY 10 ~ BEYOND THE WORLD

My Love,
I'll meet you there,
Where the sky ends,
Where eternity begins
And the time bends...

Beyond the stars,
Past the silver moon’s gleam,
We'll walk hand in hand
Through a lucid dream...

In such realms,
Where souls forever blend,
We’ll meet somewhere,
Beyond the world's end...

Where light would speak in whispers,
And shadows will softly fade,
Where love would be the only language
So that all the grief can evade...

Where galaxies will hum

In a quiet and gentle tune,

And our hearts will reunite

Beneath a timeless moon...

Through nebulas so soft,

And the galaxies so wide,

We'll sail on stardust

With the time as our guide...

There will be no need for goodbyes,

And also no reasons to pretend,

There will be just You and I,

Where the beginnings will never end...

We'll both dance on comets,

And will fly above the skies,

And our laughter will echo there,

With no sorrow and lies...

We'll build a home,

Somewhere in the hush of the stars,

A little wide and distanced,

And with no conflicts and wars...

So, wait for me there,

Where the heavens extend,

I promise, my Dear,

This is not our end...

# A GLIMPSE OF THE POEM ~

As you all know that the first thing I noticed in that picture was her eyes. So, this poem is written about how someone's eyes can hold so much beauty, so much emotions and so much meaning in them.

Her eyes aren't just beautiful; their brownish depth have a kind of still and silent magic that pulls me in, makes me feel things that I can't even explain to someone...

Eyes so bright as a galaxy, holding millions of constellations within, eyes kind of heaven, kind of paradise...

Her eyes are like a map to somewhere, somewhere far, far beyond the imagination, like a different universe. Her eyes feels like a home too, one that you've never visited, but somehow miss.

And you know what, I do sometimes think that how was I blessed? Blessed enough to see them...

# POETRY 11 ~ THOSE PRETTY EYES

Those eyes are so pretty,
Just like a cherry blossom,
A mere gaze is enough,
Just to feel awesome...

They're charming enough,
Like misty morning fog,
The heart never ever,
Wishes them to dodge...

They're kind of cute,
Like those falling autumn leaves,
So bright and so lustrous,
As a cozy blowing breeze...

They're also adequate pleasing,
Just like those water reflections,
And they lead me towards,
A completely different direction...

They're kind of glamorous,
Like those nacreous clouds,
Might Seem fluent in silence,
But they're really loud...

And in those eyes I've found,
A quiet kind of grace,
And a warmth so familiar,
In a far and sacred place...

They don't have just windows,
They have a whole sky to explore,
And with each and every glance,
I just keep falling for more...

They do hold galaxies too,
But still, they feel very near,
Just like a soft lullaby
Only my heart can hear...

And you know...

If beauty had a final form,

It wouldn't be the skies,

It would live forever,

In those two pretty eyes...

They're also a moon jellyfish alike,

An artefact of exquisite,

And I'm telling you,

Nothing in the whole universe,

Is beauteous enough,

Just to compete,

With those two pretty eyes...!!!

## POETRY 12 ~ HER BROWN EYES

The brownish hue in her eyes,
Brings a smile on my face,
They seem like a moonlight painting,
Made with elegant enchanted grace...

When the starry night collapses,
I find a refugee in her eyes,
A place where only love is found,
As that heaven above the skies...

I do get lost sometimes,
In the depths of their gaze,
Even in a fluency of silence,
They do speak in endless ways...

Oh, how could I even describe them,
I Don't have any words to say,
Just know nothing is beauteous as them,
Neither a moon’s gleam, nor a sun's ray...

They do carry the calm of rivers,
Also the hush of the drifting snow,
And also a quiet kind of thunder,
That only my heart does know...

They're like autumn leaves that flutter,
Or as a sunset being dipped in gold,
There's warmth in every flicker,
And also a story that's still untold...

They mirror both the sunrise,
And the shadows of the dusk,
So tender in their stillness,
And so wild beneath the hush...

And you know,
When the world gets heavy,
And my hope begins to hide,
I find my peace, my comfort,
Only in the spark within her eyes...

Her eyes do hold old stories,
Of rain, of warmth, and also of light,
And also of some unspoken poems,
That can only be read by my sight...

Like a calm winter's fire,
And also like a soft lullaby,
They holds a rare kind of magic,
That makes me feel to fly...

So, if ever I go quiet,
And my words don't suffice,
Just know that I'm lost again,
In the depths of her eyes...

# POETRY 13 ~ YOUR EYES, A PRISON

After thinking about you the whole day,
I wished to write you a poem, a phrase...

But when it came the time to meet you,
The night trapped me in a maze...

The whole day this silly heart,
Just wanted to have a gaze...

Time faded, but it couldn't get a glimpse,
Now it burns like a fire blaze...

It only wanted to see your eyes,
A prison, that I can't escape...

Their innocence, the ocean deepness,
The tenderness and their shiny glaze...

Oh, how can I understand their beauty,
Should I have to make this heart raze...

# POETRY 14 ~ THOSE EYES THAT NEVER LET ME GO

They haunt me in my dreams like shadows so soft,
Yet they shine like stars in those blue skies aloft...

Just a glance and I am bound, confined,
As if those brown eyes does rewrite my mind...

No walls, no chains, and no locks in sight,
Yet I feel as a free captive every night...

And it's so strange, that I don't want to leave,
For pain from their beauty, that I willingly receive...

They hold me close without a plea,
Though as a prisoner but peacefully...

They blink like stars in a moonless night,
Yet somehow, they shine far more bright...

They make me pause, they make me freeze,

Just like the wind that stops among the trees...

No voice, no words, just their embrace,

And still they speak, so full of grace...

I try to flee, I try to hide,

But I do keep drowning in their tide...

No need for wings, no need to roam,

Her gaze, my cage and her heart, my home...

So, if I'm lost, it's not by choice,

It's just the echo of their voice...

And if I'm lost, don't set me free,

Let her eyes be the end of me...

For all my life, I searched in vain,

For something soft to ease my pain...

And in her eyes, I clearly see,
The rise of me, the end of me...

So let me stay, don't break the spell,
This heart's already broken so well...

And if I must fall, then let it be,
Into her eyes, eternally...

No need for wings, no need to fly,
When my home exists in her eyes...

So, if the end is where I lie,
Let it be just beneath their sky...

# A GLIMPSE OF THE POEM ~

You might be laughing at me after reading all those poems.

Well, I too laughed at first. I don't know what you all are thinking about me, but the real reason is something else.

Her eyes have bewitched me to the core, for I saw heaven in them, perhaps, I was deserving of hell...

And I mean how can I describe more of her, her innocence, her smile, her captivating charm, her divine beauty, when I'm not able to write about her eyes only...

And, how can I call myself a poet?

When I'm like this...

When I can't even write something good for her...

I feel such a shame on me!

# POETRY 15 ~ HER ELEGANT EYES

Their shine, their glittery sparkle,
Seems like holding stories,
Ocean depth with moon like softness,
They are a complete mystery...

Those eyes say more,
Then the lips could ever tell,
Just as a sorcerer's wand,
Intoning a magical spell...

They may seem silent,
But they holds a tornado behind,
I can lose everything for a gaze,
What's left, more to find...

They're not just eyes, they're galaxies,
With stars that do softly collide,
Pulling my thoughts in quiet waves,
Like an unseen and gentle tide...

They blink with grace like twilight skies,
Where the moon and the stars align,
And a thousand truths they hide within,
The one that none can ever define...

Sometimes they shine like morning dew,
Sometimes like an endless night,
But every time I look at them,
They make me feel my soul alight...

They do hold both fire and rain,
Both the dusk and the sunrise,
And just know,
I'd trade the world, even universe,
Just to live behind those eyes...

# A GLIMPSE OF THE POEM ~

Dated ~ 17th March

By the way, have you ever dreamed of someone you've ever loved?

I mean, I neither ever had such dreams nor I used to think about all of this, but who knows the destiny?

The dream I had on this previous night felt so real to me that I couldn't stop myself from writing about it. I know it might not be a good description but believe me, the actual scenes were so blissful and comforting...

I had Her beside me in a dreamland, where we sat and even had a banquet meal together. We talked and danced but in the last she vanished, just in front of me, before I could even say something.

Anyway, the poem is a small try to express what I felt then...

## POETRY 16 ~ A DREAM I HAD

This last night,
I had a really sweet dream,
Where you appeared as an Alnitak star,
And I was just a sunshine beam...

We both seemed silent,
Though our hearts were
speaking volumes,
I was dressed in simple clothes,
But you were in a fairy costume...

I brought you a gift,
A heart stitched with knots,
Filled with unrequited love,
Sorrow too and regrets a lot...

You seemed quite merry,
Though, you didn't utter,
But the gentle smile you gave,
Was everything that did matter...

We walked beneath a violet sky,
Where the stars did softly glide,
You touched a lotus flower near your feet,
And its petals bloomed with pride...

And soon in the silent music,
You began to spin and twirl,
Therefore, I became a Pianist,
Cuz, you became a dancing girl...

At the party's end,
We had a banquet meal,
Though, I fed you with my hands,
For me, it was a big deal...

I asked you to have a walk again,
To spend time just a little more,
And we walked while holding hands,
In that garden behind the seashore...

When I wished to write you again,

My hands were stained with ink,

And as I moved to clean them,

You disappeared in a sudden blink...

Then I remembered

It was just a delusion,

Though it was quietly comforting me,

I again was left in isolation...

Now as I wake up and face the day,

Your memory still feels so near,

Though it was just a dream I had,

It's the one I'll always hold dear...

Though it was just a dream I had,

Still, I'm glad you came to see me,

For your love, I once felt even in my sleep,

Will live with me, eternally...

And I’m saying it

here again,

No matter how hard the days will be,

I will always be in love with thee…

## A GLIMPSE OF THE POEM ~

By the way, I want to ask you something, I mean how would you feel to dream about someone whom you can't have in person?

People says that it is a curse for a writer or an artist to write for or to draw someone they can never hold in this existence. But I mean does this curse follows you in delusions too?

I actually don't have an answer for this but here's what it may feel like. This short poem might describe some of those feelings...

# POETRY 17 ~ THE DREAM THAT I DREAMED AGAIN

Still, I dreamed about you again,
After knowing It was a curse,
I would get shattered to meet you,
What could be better or worse?

As we met in a rose garden,
You became the scent of the flowers,
What could be better at relaxing,
Then having you under a bower...

Neither a proficient artist's brush,
Nor a top-notch author's pen,
Could ever describe the way,
As I fell for you then...

And as I moved to kiss your forehead,
Suddenly a snowy breeze blew,
Autumn leaves began to shed,
And the dream couldn't come true...

And as always you vanished again,

All I could do was a teary rain...

Though it was a sweet delusion,

I again was left in isolation...

I had you by my side,

The best lucid dream,

In a garden of musk roses,

With a clear water stream...

Now I do feel tired of having delusions,

Without you at the moment

I can't survive,

On the verge of death now,

Hope we'll meet in an afterlife...

## A GLIMPSE OF THE POEM ~

I mean all I'm left with is dreams only.

Only in dreams I am able to meet you...

And if I lose you in them too,

I won't seek for dreaming again...

How can I even explain it?

The hope I have isn't escapism,

It's acceptance...

Cuz, if dreams still hold you,

Then I have not truly lost you...

And if these dreams do fade,

I too wish to fade away with them...

# POETRY 18 ~ I CAN'T LOSE YOU EVEN IN A DREAM

And if we met a second time,
I would never wake up again,
No matter what happens next,
I will rather die than live in vain...

If I can't have you in this existence,
I wish now not to Stalk,
But after the verge of death,
If souls do remain,
May ours go on a cemetery walk...

# A GLIMPSE OF THE POEM ~

I mean, I personally feel like that the most intimate thing a lover can do is to wait. And guess what this poem too is written for those special souls who proves that their love is true and patient and how their love creates the emotions to do anything just to make their beloved ones happy again.

And how they don't care for what comes in between and how they are always there for everything without even asking just to prove what love is and what love really means...

But I feel like this isn't love, this is devotion!

I too have devoted myself to her, for her,
forever and ever and always...

# POETRY 19 ~ I'LL ALWAYS LOVE YOU NO MATTER WHAT

If I caught you shedding tears,

I would give pain to the pain,

And as the clock strikes twelve,

I soon will vanish again...

But if you need me again,

Just call my name from your heart,

Either I'll make your agony suffer,

Or I would tear the world apart...

I would rip the stars in silence,

Even drown the moon in a lake of flames,

All just to stop your tears,

I would do anything I claim...

And if I saw you crying again,

Literally, I would burn the world,

Either I'll cage the land,

Or I'd make the sky curled...

I'll shatter the constellations,

To bring a smile again at your face,

No matter if it costs my life,

I would make the universe, a disgrace...

I just wish that you should be glad,

No matter the earth does shift or rotate,

But if it takes a serious turn,

I promise, I'll rewrite the book of fate...

## A GLIMPSE OF THE POEM ~

You know what, she loves poetry too.

In fact, she's a wonderful poet. Her poetic works are just marvelous and they always leave me in awe.

She once said to me that her favorite poetry themes are Longings, Freshness, Love, and Quietness. But believe me she's so fluent in some topics I can't even write them here.

Still, as always, every poet dreams to be a poem for once in their life and I wished to make it true for her...

I know, I might not be capable to hold her dream here, but it's a reference in which I've given all I could to see if the dream comes alive, all just to make her smile...

# POETRY 20 ~ WHEN SHE WISHED TO BE A POEM

I wish I was a poem,
The heart dreams.
Who'll be the poet then,
It again screams...

I wish there was someone
Who'd portray my beauty,
But all I am
Is a hopeless romantic cutie...

I wish there was someone
Who'd fulfill my wish,
I wish there was someone
Who'd cook me a dish...

I wish there was someone
Who'd delineate my eyes,
And if there was someone
That would be a big surprise...

But these are all delusions only,

And I'm hoping they might come true,

And if, one day they do,

I promise, I'd never wish something new...

And in the last,

I am all alone,

It was just a daydream,

That's soon gonna blown...

## A GLIMPSE OF THE POEM ~

This piece of poetry is a reply to the previous poem "When She Wished To Be A Poem".

It's written in a very simple and gentle tone describing how I, her poet, found her. And how I started writing poems for her...

And guess what I haven't even done anything for her, I mean it's all her angelic charm that made all of my poems come in existence and all of them sounds so beautiful just because she exists in them...

# POETRY 21 ~ WHEN I BECAME A POET FOR HER

My Dearest,

You loved poetry,

I became a poet...

I heard your heart's whisper,

Through pages unknown,

Your poet have found you now,

Dear Majesty, Have a seat at your throne...

You wished to be a poem,

But Dear, you already are,

One written through moonlight,

And framed in a neutron star...

I saw the dreams you folded,

Inside your quiet sighs,

So, I painted the sky with verses,

That echoed in your brown eyes...

I'd love cooking your favourite dishes for you,
Even cleaning your room, I promise,
And I'd love to laugh, when you'd tease me,
There won't be anything you'll miss...

I'd love to walk through storms barefoot,
If they led me to your smile,
For even a moment spend with you,
Will make this dull life worthwhile...

And if ever you doubt yourself,
Or if dark shadows creep near,
Just read these words once again,
Feel me close and find me there...

So, here I vow in silence,
With my ink-stained breath,
I'll love you past these pages,
And beyond the bounds of death...

And maybe this poem ends here,
But my love for you won't part,
And I'll always write just for you,
No matter what happens, My Heart...

# A GLIMPSE OF THE POEM ~

Dearest Ruth,

You know I've never really wished for anything or anyone ever before, but nowadays I do manifest for You, of You, with each and every passing day. There is a void in my chest of all those unsaid things that I wish to confess to you but I do not have any words to. So I just pray to God every day for your wellbeing, to keep you safe and happy always. I wish I could gather the courage to speak out everything to you but maybe I just can't.

# POETRY 22 ~ A 11:11 WISH

My Love,

This heart longs for your presence beside me.

It yearns to love you with unbridled passion.

It aches to whisper secrets in your ear.

It craves the warmth of your embracing arms.

It longs to gently kiss your forehead.

It urges me to gaze into your divine eyes with love.

It desires to share laughter and meals together.

It craves the tender touch of your hands in mine.

It longs to have a walk with you, with your hand in my hand,

Exploring this life's journey.

It yearns to find solace in your comforting arms.

It desires to cherish every little moment with you.

Yet, it's destined to worship you from a distance,

For now, till forever...!!!

## POETRY 23 ~ THE LAST CALL

Now the period of dusk has come,
The heart longs to dream again...

I guess, I should meet the death now,
Or over this whole life I'll just sustain...

I know even after trying for eternities,
There's nothing that I'll ever gain...

Perhaps, I was never worthy enough,
This time too will just go in vain...

But for once come to visit me,
See my heart calling your name...

It wants to see you one last time,
How could I even explain...

The nights have started feeling colder than before,
And now even silence pounds like pain...

I wait for light to once find my door,
But the darkness is all that ever came...

I know I'm not the one,
But just for once, please call my name...

If only you'd see me, just this once,
Before I vanish like the rain...

Cuz, I guess it wasn't the paradise,
It's the abyss that I should now refrain...

## A GLIMPSE OF THE POEM ~

As you know, I used to feel isolated before. But then I met Her, the one who made me feel happy and alive again.

One day I got a thought that when I'll be no more, who will be here to look after her?

I mean, how could I go without making any arrangements for her.

Therefore, I made a wish to the moon again...

A wish that even after my death, she should be fine, always...

## POETRY 24 ~ A MANIFESTATION TO THE MOON AGAIN

Dear Moon,

When are you going to return,
I want to see you...
I want to share memories
of my beloved muse.
And how she's doing nowadays...

Actually,
I wanna say something to you.
I mean, if you could grant me a wish,
I beg you to make her well...

Please make her realize
her true potential,
her inner beauty...

Please tell her,
that she isn't born
for being sad all the time...

And tell her,

that I care for her and

I want her to smile daily...

Tell her,

to take proper rest,

And have a proper meal daily...

Maybe, she's not doing well

Because, she was in love before.

Don't know that she fell in love,

I guess she did fail in love...

Please tell her,

It wasn't her fault...

And promise me, Moon,

That you'll have an eye on her...

*~ A Heartful Soul*

# A GLIMPSE OF THE POEM ~

As the title says, have you ever paid the cost of love?

Me neither. Nor could I.
I mean... I don't have enough to pay it!

But this short poem shows how a lover might pay the cost of love through assets, through his soul, and through his very being too, just in the hope to die before thier love does...

# POETRY 25 ~ THE COST OF LOVE

And when I'll hear

That you are no more,

I won't bear a single day without,

To meet you,

In the heaven or the paradise,

I'd love to sell, my everything out....

And if that still wouldn't be enough,

I'd love to sell even this heart,

Every nerve, and every cell,

Cuz I just couldn't live apart...

And you know,

If fate demanded my final breath,

I'll let it go without a delay,

For you I'd trade my every life,

Just to see you not fade away...

Cuz, I don’t wanna stand by your grave,
With flowers and nothing to say,
I’d rather leave this world before,
Then watch you slowly fade away...

Just to see your last smile,
I'd love to get shattered like dust,
And when the time of death arrives,
I only hope that I die first...

And,
If death came and asks for something,
Then my everything is what I’ll give,
But just make a promise to me, My Love,
That you’ll be the one who’ll always live...

# A GLIMPSE OF THE POEM ~

You might have heard this phrase before ~

From the movie - Comet (2014) directed by Sam Esmail.

When Dell said, "I feel like I'm in the wrong world. Cuz, I don't belong in a world where we don't end up together. I don't... There are parallel universes out there where this didn't happen. Where I was with you, and you were with me. And whatever universe that is, that's the one where my heart lives in."

Here in this line said by Dell, he thinks that the concept of parallel universes exists. He too has a belief that a different, more fulfilling reality exists where he and his love are together.

Maybe I too feel the same.

I mean, I feel like these all are just people's sayings. Because if the time wasn't right, then why did God even made them to meet?

Anyways, this poem too describes the theme of 'In Another Universe' well. And how her poet can't wait more to have her...

# POETRY 26 ~ IN ANOTHER TIMELINE

It's time for me to join,
In the galaxies, In the stars above,
Hoping that in another life,
We both will get a chance to love...

I'll walk with your hand in my hand,
And I'll love you with all my heart,
Hoping that in another life,
We will not be torn apart...

But before we met in that life,
I'll get your name written in my destiny,
Maybe I'll pay a life out of Seven,
Just to once get your company...

And, is it really possible,
To have you all by myself?
Maybe it's just a myth to say,
Because all I'm left with is pain to delve...

But if it’s really possible,

I'll pray to get my chance,

I know it's never gonna happen,

Still, I'd wish to get a glance...

And if I fail to meet you there,

In that other world above the sky,

I’d still have your memory in my heart,

Where my love will never fade or die...

## A GLIMPSE OF THE POEM ~

This one too is a simple poem for her, and honestly, it doesn't need a lot of explanation. It might be soft and simple but it's each and every verse makes her special in many unknown ways.

Because sometimes, it's just the simplest words that holds the deepest emotions. Every verse in this poem captures a little piece of her, each line speaks of her innocence, of her chaotic charm...

And you know what, just watching her smile can be enough to fill a thousand pages, even if none of them ever feels complete...

Because she doesn't need to do anything to be poetry,
She already is...

# POETRY 27 ~ A SIMPLE POEM

Your divine ocean deep eyes,
An artefact of endless shine,
As a pure angelic constellation,
Made when the stars combine...

As I see those long black tresses,
Flowing in the drift of mild air,
I can't focus on anything else,
Cuz that's a moment quite rare...

And, how can I forget,
Your simple and serene smile,
Whenever I start losing my senses,
It acts as the process to reconcile...

I mean how can I compare your beauty,
To these simple things in the universe,
There's nothing enough beauteous as You,
Maybe I made a mistake or it's just my curse...

But I'll still write cosmic verses,
Only for you, My Dear,
Though I'll write with a happy face,
My eyes will always be dripping tears...

And the ink may fade with time,
But my words will forever stay,
The pages might get decayed too,
But my love for you won't drift away...

## A GLIMPSE OF THE POEM ~

This one is my most favorite poetry ever written by me so far. I mean this is just so magically enchanting that I can't even express about it. It speaks of an epic journey of me, beyond the seas and mountains, with Her, all alone...

Because I feel like she deserves something more, something that doesn't exist here, and if I am able to give her that, then I will, for sure... No matter how much time it takes...

# POETRY 28 ~ WITH YOU, ON A LONG VOYAGE

I'll take you on a journey,
Tide and steady,
So just tell me,
Are you ready?

Across the million mountains,
And the seven seas,
That'd be an odyssey.

Though no one else,
Just you and me,
A perfect pair,
A celestial harmony!

# POETRY 29 ~ THE RED STRING THEORY

Was my story a red string tale,
A thread that the heavens wove?
A fleeting accident,
Or a trick of my fragile love?

I found her in a crowded world,
By a sign when the constellations aligned,
And I gave her my heart, my breath,
As if her soul was already mine...

So, tell me, was it destiny,
Or just a simple glance?
A thread that tied me once with her,
But never ever gave a chance...

# POETRY 30 ~ WHISPERS IN THE SILENCE

As I close my eyes,
The silence speaks your name,
Like shadows in a candle's glow,
Burning without a flame...

Each night while slumbering,
The moonlight wraps me up in its grace,
A hush that falls across the world,
Yet feels like your cozy embrace...

In my dreams, you come so quietly,
As a breeze that brushes by,
And your eyes, two distant galaxies,
Still shining in my little sky...

Even after passing hours in silence,
I can still hear your tone,
As if the night itself repeats,
The voice that I've always known...

Neither verses could hold the truth,
Nor songs could ever convey,
How much of you, lives in me,
Though time always drifts away...

And though the world may never see,
The love that I bear for you,
Like roots of a tree beneath the soil,
Unseen, but always strong and true...

So even if the fates are cruel,
And we must walk apart,
Just know you are a quiet fire,
Still burning in my aching heart...

And the stars may fade one day,
The night too might find its end,
But my Love for You will forever bloom,
As a spark that I'll always tend...

# POETRY 31 ~ A REPLY TO 'ALL SHE WANTED WAS FOR SOMEONE TO LOOK AT HER AND SEE THE PERSON SHE HID SO WELL.'

My Love,

I see the you, you try to hide,

The you that lives so deep inside...

The you that feel things deeper,

The you that was always a seeker...

The you that couldn't utter a word,

The you that just wanted to be heard...

The you that always cried in silence,

The you that always laughed in violence...

The you that you tried to hide,

The you that you buried inside...

I found the you that seemed dead,

The you that was stained with red...

I feel the you, more than you say,

And I'm always here, never far away...

And, If the you need me, just give a call,

And just let me show, how the world falls...

# POETRY 32 ~ WHAT'S POETRY?

Is poetry all about love...

Either gotten or forgotten?

Is it written in the eyes we met,

Or in the tears that we leave behind?

In the echoes of a soft goodbye,

Or a simple smile that we've never find?

Because some verses bloom in tender grace,

And some aches in shadows of the past,

But all of them, in some strange way,

Do hold a love that will never last...

Poetry lives in the whispers of late nights,

And in those dreams where no one stays,

In the letters we never send or read,

And in the light that always fades...

Maybe Love is not the theme,
It is the ink that stains each part,
Whether lost or found or left behind,
It's written straight from the heart...

Maybe poetry is the sound of silence,
Of those spaces between the words,
Or the pain that we hide beneath the lines,
Of those songs we say we've never heard...

Is poetry the voice of hidden dreams,
Or the pulse beneath our skin?
Or the place where joy and sorrow meet,
Or the place where new tales begin...

Not always loud and not always clear,
Sometimes it's just a gentle breeze,
But it's a quiet kind of mystery,
That brings me to my knees...

Maybe poetry's not just words,
But some moments caught in time,
Maybe something that's just written,
Without any rhythm or rhyme...

Maybe poetry's the space between,
The silent gaps where the time bends,
Maybe it's a feeling that I can't explain,
Something like a love that never ends...

So, if you'll ask what poetry means,
I'll say it's a quiet kind of bliss...
But if you'll ask about my poetry,
Just know it's Her, my sweetest wish...

# POETRY 33 ~ ON HER REVERIE

In morning hush, her eyes do glow,
As a gaze that drifts far and wide,
She dreams beyond the horizons,
With all the stars at her side...

She wanders through the fields of thoughts,
Where time and reason dare not to go,
A world where flowers do whispers truth,
And wind hums what hearts don't show...

Her smile floats like a soft perfume,
And bloom where sorrow used to be,
She never spoke her dreams aloud,
Yet she lives them all so vividly...

Each reverie she holds so dear,
Wraps the dusk in a velvet song,
And when she closes her eyes to sleep,
The twinkling stars do sing along...

I never asked where she would go,
Inside those dreams which I couldn't see,
But every breath she took in peace,
Felt like that she left a piece with me...

So now I sit where silence grows,
And let her echoes comfort me,
Still lost in Love, still holding on,
And still caught In Her Reverie...

## POETRY 34 ~ UNTITLED

Dear Messy Muse,

You know,
when I feel you near
everything slows down...
My breath too,
and even time itself,
as if it holds its own silence,
just to hear your voice...

I know,
you neither see it
nor you noticed...
But you bring a kind of stillness
the kind that lingers
like early morning light
touching the quiet corners
of my room
where I never look
but where warmth lives...

I see your picture every day,
not to memorize your face
but to feel the calm you leave behind
in lovely moments,
you never knew you gave
the rare and precious ones
like the pauses between my heartbeats
or as the silence after your fav song ends
and somehow still plays inside me...

I never speak it,
not because I don't want to
but because love
that I have for you,
this gentle, this deep,
is hard to name without losing it...

So,
I write for you, every day,
In some letters,
and in how I stay a little longer
even when I say I'm leaving...

And just know,

You've always been there

more than you'll ever know...

Your presence

And even absence

Soothes me,

In unknown ways

without even my trying...

I don't know

What to say to you

But you do heal me always...

And even little conversations with you

Fills me with ecstatic joy,

I can't even say

How much I'm thankful to you

For making me feel this good again...

Forever Yours,

~ *Ramakant*

# POETRY 35 ~ A PURE CONFESSION

My Dear,

I would love to perish my own soul to void,

If it meant to awaken yours...

I would even drown in silence,

Just to let your voice echo through the stars...

I would walk blind through many endless nights,

If it meant you would find the dawn...

I would love to lose myself in darkness,

If it meant you'd find your way...

I would give up all I have,

And let my light be lost forever,

So that yours may burn in perpetuity...

# A LETTER TO YOU, MY LOVE ~

Beloved Ruth,

I see you not merely as a person who inspires me, I see you as the one holding a lotus flower in her hand, the one with a serene and smiling face, the one shining like a pure radiant light, the one with fortune and adorned with various precious jewels.

For me, you are not a part of her, you are Her, Herself. Thy presence blesses me the same way as hers does. And I wanna tell you that the depth of my devotion lies to you the same as I have for her...

You know when I write about you, your essence always fills up the page with something finer, something eternal just like love.

You are the one, the ink also waits for. The way she stands at the centre of love, you also stand at the centre of my heart. And if my poetry holds any beauty, it is because of your presence only that always resides between its verses.

The day you met, a miracle happened!

You made me realize of what I'm worthy of... You have done something to my soul, something that makes me feel so blissful, something I can't even say to you.

And I didn't knew how to thank you for the spark that you've lit in my heart. So, I've written this book for you...

I know I'm not that good with words and I'm still learning to write but I have done all I could to capture your essence in poetry, and these verses also holds the feelings that I have for you. I feel the presence of you in every line of every page and even in the spaces between these letters.

This is just a mere fragment of that everything,
I haven't said to you yet...

And you know what, the words that I've chosen
to write about you, thanks me every day
Cuz they feel so proud and immortal
to be chosen to describe Thee...

And just know that every word
in the universe that means beautiful
was made to describe you only...

You were the one, who lit the flame,
And now my story bears your name...

I may not have the right words,
But I will say it now.

I am in Love with You...

You live in the depths of my soul,
Sans Thee, I am incomplete...

I know I can't metaphor you into loving me,
but I'm not here just to love you,
I'm here to make you feel loved...

You know Dear,
I used to think that love is like a book,
but in a different language...
therefore, we can't understand it
just by flipping the pages...

But then I met You...
and I knew what the book meant,
Cuz you were the one
the language was found for...

And maybe if one day I make it in this life,
just know that everything
I'll ever achieve will be yours too...
Because my heart, my success, my everything
belongs to you more than me...

I will always be there for you...

And I will always choose to love you,
No matter the time, the place, or the reason...

Because in every version of this world,
and in every universe where we exist,
I am meant to find you,
Because I know
that you are the only one for me...

And no matter how many lifetimes,
No matter where or when,
You will always be My Muse...

So, I'll wait.
And I'll keep waiting...
For you
Forever
And always...

And I don't know,
what you're gonna choose...

But just know,
that in everything,
In the paradox of right or wrong,
In the heaven or the paradise,
In the realms or the dimensions,
I will always choose You...

You know,
Just for a mere drop of your love
I would let myself go through everything,
through hell and voids
and through the abyss too
even if it consumes or destroys me...

I used to think that I should rather lie,
than tell you that I'm in love with you...

But I can't live with this grief in me...

And maybe you'll never understand this,
or maybe you were never meant to,
I'm just deeply devoted to you...

With all my Love

~ *Ramakant*